HANNAH MONTANA

TO:

Good times, good friends.
What more does a girl need?

FROM:

© Disney

HANNAH MONTANA

TO:

You rock my world!
Happy Valentine's Day!

FROM:

HANNAH MONTANA

TO:

U R 100% QL!*
(*You are totally cool!!)
Happy Valentine's Day!

FROM:

HANNAH MONTANA

TO:

Life's picture perfect
with you by my side!
Glad we're pals!

FROM:

It's usually the people who've known you the longest who know you the best. Glad we're friends!

TO:

FROM:

BFF!*

(*Best Friends Forever!)
Happy Valentine's Day!

TO:

FROM:

Thanks for keeping my feet on the ground! Happy Valentine's Day!

TO:

FROM:

Happy Valentine's Day! Ya think?

TO:

FROM:

When life gets stressful,
it's good to get silly!
Happy Valentine's Day!

TO:

FROM:

U R D GR8st!*

(*You are the greatest!)
Happy Valentine's Day!

TO:

FROM:

Even when we just hang out,
I always have fun with you!
Happy Valentine's Day!

TO:

FROM:

Happy Valentine's Day
from your biggest fan!

TO:

FROM:

I'm glad you don't take me too seriously. Happy Valentine's Day!

TO:

FROM:

U R 2G2BT!*

(*You are too good to be true!)

TO:

FROM:

Happy Valentine's Day! What, you thought I forgot?

TO:

FROM:

I'm glad I have you to hang with, 'cause life is *never* dull! Happy Valentine's Day!

TO:

FROM:

HANNAH MONTANA

TO:

Thanks for being my biggest fan (even though I know you'd never admit it)!

FROM:

HANNAH MONTANA

TO:

TAY!*

(*Thinking about you!)
Happy Valentine's Day!

FROM:

HANNAH MONTANA

TO:

I'm glad you're always waiting in the wings to back me up. Happy Valentine's Day!

FROM:

HANNAH MONTANA

TO:

Thanks for always being there for me. Happy Valentine's Day!

FROM:

TO:

You've always got my back,
and I've got yours!

FROM:

TO:

Someone should write a song
about how cool you are!
Happy Valentine's Day!

FROM:

TO:

You don't have to be
a pop star to rock!
Happy Valentine's Day!

FROM:

TO:

Sweet niblets! Is it
Valentine's Day already?
Don't worry, I gotcha covered.

FROM:

There's nothing more important
than our friendship.
Happy Valentine's Day!

TO:

FROM:

Happy Valentine's Day
to a superstar!

TO:

FROM:

I'd never make it through
Valentine's Day without
a friend like you!

TO:

FROM:

You know what?
We'll be friends forever!
Happy Valentine's Day!

TO:

FROM:

HANNAH MONTANA

HANNAH MONTANA

TO:

Can you keep a secret?
I think you're pretty cool!

FROM:

HANNAH MONTANA

TO:

We should hang out more often.
Happy Valentine's Day!

FROM:

HANNAH MONTANA

TO:

It's Valentine's Day?
For real? Have a good one.

FROM:

HANNAH MONTANA

TO:

From one superstar to another . . .
Happy Valentine's Day!

FROM:

TO:

Even when you're a big dork
like me, you gotta luck out
sometimes. I sure did
when I met you!

FROM:

TO:

Life's golden with
a friend like you!
Happy Valentine's Day!

FROM:

TO:

U R GR8T! XOXO*

(*You're great! Hugs and kisses.)

FROM:

TO:

Who needs stardom when
you've got friends like this?

FROM:

TO:

UR 2 QL 4 Words!*

(*You are too cool for words!)

FROM:

You ready to rock this Valentine's Day?

TO:

FROM:

© Disney

Happy Valentine's Day, y'all!

TO:

FROM:

© Disney

You've got some wicked tricks— but the best one is that you always know how to cheer me up! Glad we're buds.

TO:

FROM:

© Disney

TO:

I'm glad I've got you to keep me focused on what really matters! Happy Valentine's Day!

FROM:

© Disney

TO:

I'm glad we're friends. Happy Valentine's Day!

FROM:

© Disney

TO:

You're a megahit to me! Happy Valentine's Day!

FROM:

© Disney

TO:

You're just like a song— you get stuck in my head! Happy Valentine's Day!

FROM:

© Disney

HANNAH MONTANA

TO:

It's good to know that you'll always
think of me as your little sis'.
Happy Valentine's Day!

FROM:

HANNAH MONTANA

Valentine's Day is landing in
three . . . two . . . one.
Have a good one!

TO:

FROM:

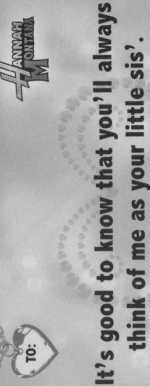

HANNAH MONTANA

Make some noise!
Have a rockin'
Valentine's Day!

TO:

FROM:

HANNAH MONTANA

Time to chill—it's
Valentine's Day!

TO:

FROM:

TO:

I can't believe you're my friend—I'm the luckiest girl ever! Happy Valentine's Day!

FROM:

TO:

The best of both worlds? Having a friend like you!

FROM:

TO:

Sometimes, the best days are when we just hang out . . . Happy Valentine's Day!

FROM:

XOXO! Happy Valentine's Day!

FROM:

HANNAH MONTANA

I couldn't imagine celebrating Valentine's Day without you.

Glad we're buds!

TO:

FROM:

HANNAH MONTANA

I might be rockin', but you're pretty cool, too. Happy Valentine's Day!

TO:

FROM:

HANNAH MONTANA

Friends 4EAE!* (*Friends Forever and Ever!) Happy Valentine's Day!

TO:

FROM:

HANNAH MONTANA

Your smile makes the day go faster! Glad we're pals!

TO:

FROM:

HANNAH MONTANA

TO:

I feel like I can tell you anything. Glad we're pals! Happy Valentine's Day!

FROM:

HANNAH MONTANA

TO:

It's always good to have a friend who likes you more than they like their favorite pop star!

FROM:

HANNAH MONTANA

TO:

Friends 4Ever! Happy Valentine's Day!

FROM:

HANNAH MONTANA

TO:

What a coinkydink—I got you a valentine, too! Happy Valentine's Day!

FROM:

Happy Valentine's Day to a superspecial friend!

TO:

FROM:

I'm glad we're related—it keeps me on my toes! Happy Valentine's Day!

TO:

FROM:

You rock! Happy Valentine's Day!

TO:

FROM:

U R 2 QL!* (*You are too cool!) Happy Valentine's Day!

TO:

FROM: